The Deep, Deep, Deep Puddle

Mary Jessie Parker

illustrated by
Deborah Zemke

DIAL BOOKS FOR YOUNG READERS
an imprint of Penguin Group (USA), Inc.

For Boots and his best friend, Jim
—M.J.P.

For my mom and dad
—D.Z.

DIAL BOOKS FOR YOUNG READERS

A division of Penguin Young Readers Group • Published by The Penguin Group • Penguin Group (USA) Inc., 375 Hudson Street, New York, NY 10014, U.S.A. • Penguin Group (Canada), 90 Eglinton Avenue East, Suite 700, Toronto, Ontario, Canada M4P 2Y3 (a division of Pearson Penguin Canada Inc.) • Penguin Books Ltd, 80 Strand, London WC2R 0RL, England • Penguin Ireland, 25 St. Stephen's Green, Dublin 2, Ireland (a division of Penguin Books Ltd) • Penguin Group (Australia), 250 Camberwell Road, Camberwell, Victoria 3124, Australia (a division of Pearson Australia Group Pty Ltd) • Penguin Books India Pvt Ltd, 11 Community Centre, Panchsheel Park, New Delhi - 110 017, India • Penguin Group (NZ), 67 Apollo Drive, Rosedale, Auckland 0632, New Zealand (a division of Pearson New Zealand Ltd) • Penguin Books (South Africa) (Pty) Ltd, 24 Sturdee Avenue, Rosebank, Johannesburg 2196, South Africa • Penguin Books Ltd, Registered Offices: 80 Strand, London WC2R 0RL, England

Designed by Mina Chung and Irene Vandervoort • Text set in Mr Eaves Sans • Manufactured in China on acid free paper

2 4 6 8 10 9 7 5 3 1

Library of Congress Cataloging-in-Publication Data

Parker, Mary Jessie.
The deep deep puddle / by Mary Jessie Parker ; illustrated by Deborah Zemke.   p. cm.
Summary: During an overnight rainstorm, a large and deep puddle forms across a city street, and the next day increasing numbers of creatures or things disappear into it, from one shaggy dog to nine robbers.
ISBN 978-0-8037-3765-5 (hardcover)
[1. Rain and rainfall—Fiction. 2. Counting.] I. Zemke, Deborah, ill. II. Title.
PZ7.P22735De 2013   [E]—dc23   2012017259

This art was created using gouache on Fabriano Artistico paper.

On a busy street
in the late afternoon,
the rain begins.

Through the long night
and the early morn,
the rain falls.

A puddle . . .

a deep,
deep puddle
swells
and stretches
across the city street.

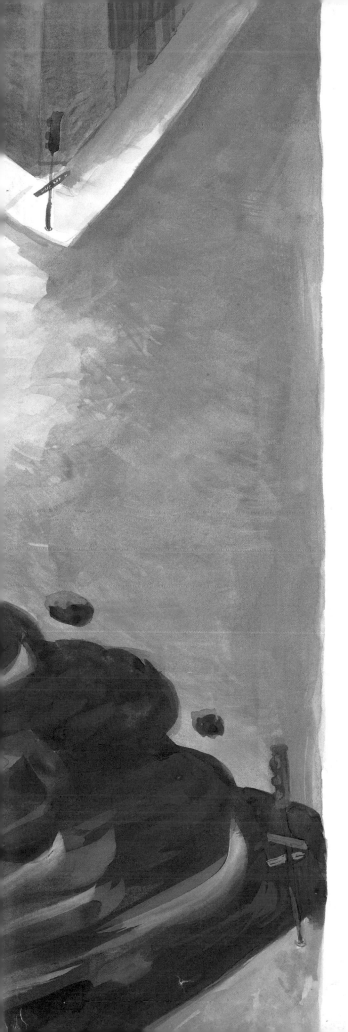

One shaggy dog,
soaked from the rain,
wanders and sniffs
a little too close
to the edge of the deep,
deep puddle
and . . .

Glub...

Glub...

Glub...

he sinks

out of

sight.

Two

stray cats
track curious
reflections
a little too close
to the edge of
the deep,
deep puddle
and . . .

Glub...

Glub...

Glub...

they sink

out of

sight.

Three thirsty squirrels leap-hop, leap-hop,

Four pigeons tap-a-tap-tap for seeds,

Five children, late for school, splash and dash,

Six

tourists tangle
camera straps and maps
a little too close
to the edge of
the deep,
deep puddle
and . . .

Glub...
Glub...
Glub...

they all sink

out of

sight.

Seven taxis

cruise for fares,

Eight

street vendors
rush to
curbside spots,

Nine robbers,

coats crammed with stolen treasures,
prowl a little too close to the edge of
the deep, deep puddle
and . . .

Glub...
Glub...
Glub...

they all sink
out of
sight.

Ten
police officers
converge at the edge
of the deep,
deep puddle and . . .

Halt.

They cordon off the deep, deep puddle with yellow caution tape and call for help.

Eleven

tanker trucks park behind the tape.

Twelve

workers crank long hoses
into the deep, deep puddle and . . .

Schlurp!

Schlurp!

Schlurp!

The deep, deep puddle . . .

disappears!

Twelve workers stuff long hoses in

Eleven tanker trucks, and drive away as

Ten police officers restore order as

Nine robbers are arrested as

Eight street vendors sell snacks and souvenirs as

Seven taxis pull up to the curb as

Six tourists hail a ride as

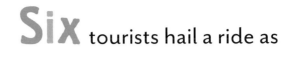

Five children dump soggy sack lunches as

Four pigeons pick and peck as

Three squirrels pack cheeks
with bits of soggy bread as

Two stray cats fuss and hiss as

One

shaggy dog,
soaked from a long night
and early morn of rain,
and the deep,
deep puddle . . .

stands . . .

a new puddle,
a new
deep,
deep puddle,
swells
and stretches
across the city
street.